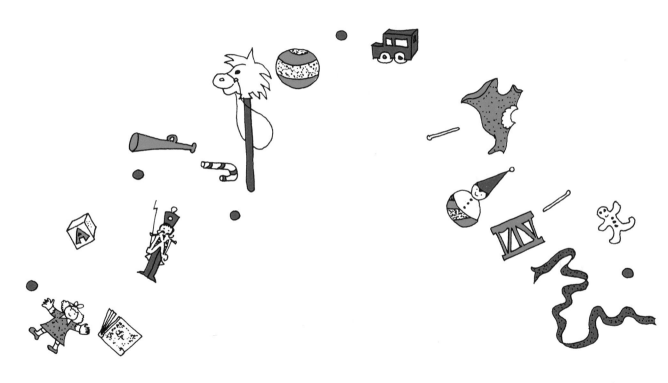

What Did You Lose, Santa?

BY BERTHE AMOSS

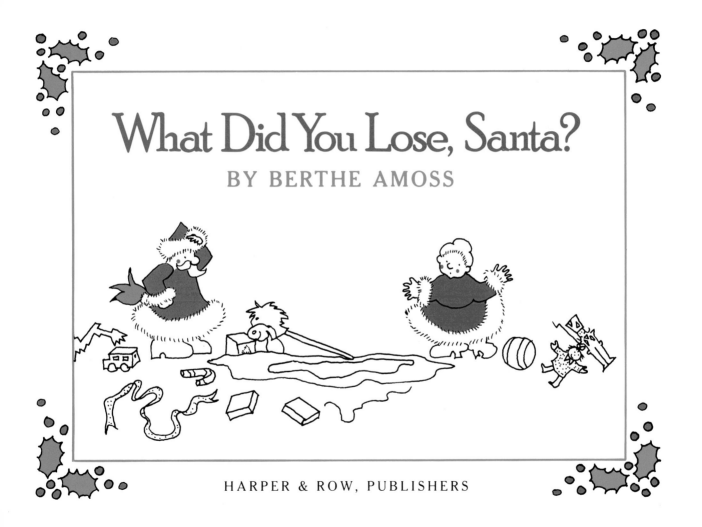

HARPER & ROW, PUBLISHERS

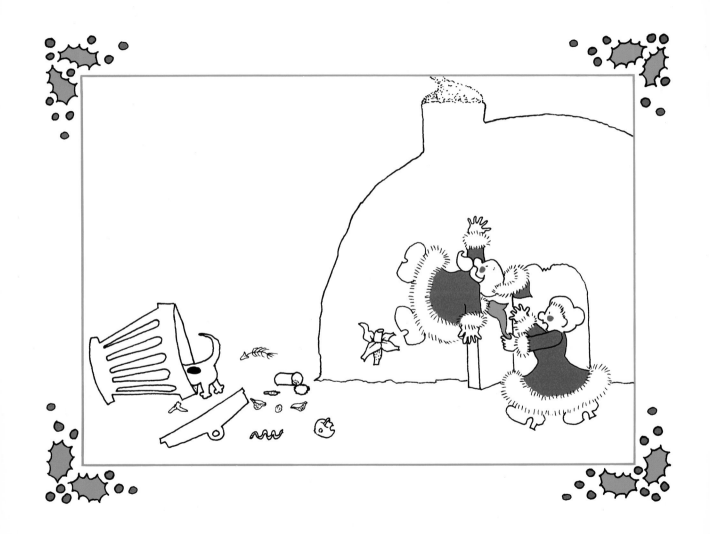

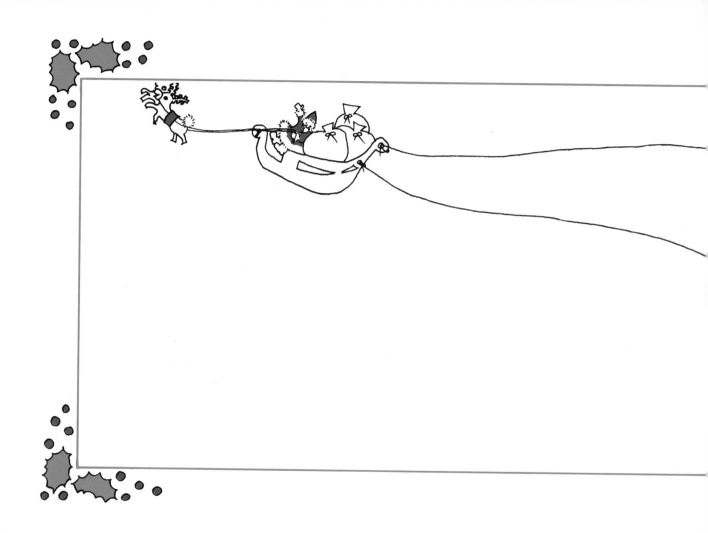

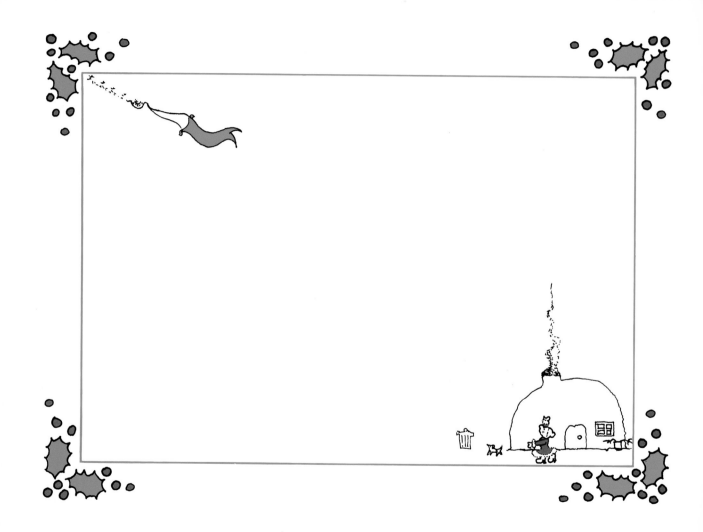

What Did You Lose, Santa?
Copyright © 1987 by Berthe Amoss
Printed in Singapore. All rights reserved.
1   2   3   4   5   6   7   8   9   10
First Edition

Library of Congress Cataloging-in-Publication Data
Amoss, Berthe.
   What did you lose, Santa?

   Summary: Santa searches high and low before he
finds the "Peace on Earth" banner he plans to trail
behind his sleigh.
   1. Santa Claus—Juvenile fiction. [1. Santa Claus—
Fiction. 2. Christmas—Fiction. 3. Lost and found
possessions—Fiction. 4. Stories without words]
I. Title.
PZ7.A5177Wh 1987   [E]   86-33633
ISBN 0-694-00197-X